TRUN

MR BOUNCER'S
HOUSE

FIRE
STATION

BLODGER'S
GATEHOUSE

SIGMUND SWAMP'S
HOUSE & BOATHOUSE

FERNYBANK FERRY

BROCK GRUFFY'S
SHOP

BRAMBLE'S FARM

CHURCH

VICARAGE

RAILWAY STATION

P.C. HOPPIT'S
HOUSE

POLICE
STATION

DR. BUSHY'S
HOUSE

N
W E
S

This book belongs to:

....

PUBLISHED BY PETER HADDOCK LIMITED, BRIDLINGTON, ENGLAND.
© FERN HOLLOW PRODUCTIONS LIMITED.

MRS. MERRYWEATHER'S LETTER

Written and Illustrated by John Patience

ph

Mrs Merryweather, who lived in Poppletown, had just
finished writing a long letter to her friend in Fern Hollow.
She signed the letter with a flourish of her quill pen,

> Your very dear friend

> Matilda Merryweather.

P.S. The weather here is wonderful — it is raining cats and
dogs!

Putting up her umbrella the happy duck splashed her way along the street to the postbox. The raindrops made little bubbles in the puddles and the oil from the traffic made rainbow patterns in the streams which ran down the gutters. Mrs Merryweather began to sing:

> "Quack, quack the rain pours down
> This is the weather for me
> Let it patter and pour
> And drizzle galore
> And a happy duck I shall be."

"Off you go," she said, popping the letter into the box, and she waddled back home again.

By the next morning Mrs Merryweather's letter was in Mr Periwinkle's postbag, along with all the other letters he had to deliver. The weather in Fern Hollow was very windy, and Mr Periwinkle was having considerable trouble in pedalling his bicycle. Suddenly as he turned the corner by Boris Blink's bookshop, a great gust of wind caught him and

blew him over. The letters spilled out of his bag and blew
away down the street. The poor postman hurried after
them and managed to catch all but one, and that was
Mrs Merryweather's letter; away it sailed, high over the
rooftops.

At the watermill, Mr Croaker was busy loading his barge with sacks of flour, which he would later take to Poppletown. The most difficult part of the job was walking along the plank from the riverbank on to the barge. This required a good sense of balance. Unfortunately Mr Croaker completely lost his, when Mrs Merryweather's letter blew by right under his nose. Thinking the letter might be something important, Mr Croaker made a snatch at it and the next moment he found himself in the river. Mrs Merryweather's letter seemed to hover above him for a second and then it danced away on the wind over the tops of the trees.

Farmer Bramble emptied the bucket of swill into the pigs'
trough. "Eat up," he said. Grunting with pleasure, the pigs
began to gobble up the food. Just then, out of the corner of
his eye, Farmer Bramble caught sight of something fluttering
by. It was Mrs Merryweather's letter. "I wonder if that's for
me?" he cried. Leaping over the wall of the sty, he grabbed a
pitchfork and rushed after the letter, trying to catch it on the
prongs of the fork. But Farmer Bramble quickly ran out of
breath and puffed his way back to the pig sty, where he
found he had left the gate open and all the pigs had run
away!

Mr Chips was busy painting the front of Brock Gruffy's shop, when along came Sigmund Swamp who was in a rather daydreamy sort of mood. Sigmund didn't notice Mr Chips and walked right under his ladder. That was very unlucky. At that moment Mrs Merryweather's letter came floating by and blew right into Mr. Chips's face. The startled beaver almost slipped off his ladder and dropped his can of paint, which fell down with a great blue splash on top of Sigmund's head!

All that day Mrs Merryweather's letter blew around the village. Lots of people tried to catch it but no-one succeeded. At last, as evening came, the wind dropped and the letter fluttered down to rest in a bird's nest. The bird itself was fast asleep and didn't notice the letter slip quietly in beside it.

When the bird woke up
the next morning, it was
very annoyed to see the letter
cluttering up its nest and quickly
tossed it out. Airborne again,
Mrs Merryweather's letter went
fluttering over the railway station
where, just then, a train was
arriving. And who should step
out of one of the carriages but
Mrs Merryweather. The duck didn't
notice her letter flying by, but
handed her ticket to Mr Twinkle
and waddled out of the station.

Mrs Willowbank was up to her elbows in soapy water as she scrubbed away at her washing. Suddenly, through the open window, in blew Mrs Merryweather's letter. Mrs Willowbank

picked up the letter and saw that it was addressed to her!
"It's from Matilda," she cried, reading the letter. "She's
coming to visit me this morning." As she spoke there was
a knock at the door. It was Mrs Merryweather herself.
"I see you got my letter," she said. "Yes," replied
Mrs Willowbank. "It arrived by airmail!"
Soon the two friends were sharing a pot of tea and a lovely
plum cake and wondering how on earth the letter had
managed to deliver itself without any help from the postman!

Fern Hollow

MR. CHIPS'S HOUSE

MR. WILLOWBANK'S COBBLER'S SHOP

MR. CROAKER'S WATERMILL

STRIPEY'S HOUSE

SCHOOL

RIVER FERNY

THE JOLLY VOLE HOTEL

MR. ACORN'S BAKERY

MR. RUSTY'S HOUSE

MR. PRICKLESS HOUSE

POST OFFICE

BORIS BLINKS'S BOOKSHOP

MR. TWINKLE'S HOUSE

MR. TUTTLEEBEE'S SHOP

MR. THIMBLE'S TAILORS SHOP

WINDYWOOD